William's Ninth Life

story by Minna Jung
pictures by Vera Rosenberry

Orchard Books   New York

Text copyright © 1993 by Minna Jung
Illustrations copyright © 1993 by Vera Rosenberry
All rights reserved. No part of this book may be reproduced or transmitted in any form or by
any means, electronic or mechanical, including photocopying, recording, or by any information
storage or retrieval system, without permission in writing from the Publisher.

Orchard Books, 95 Madison Avenue, New York, NY 10016

Manufactured in the United States of America. Printed by Barton Press, Inc.
Bound by Horowitz/Rae. Book design by Mina Greenstein.
The text of this book is set in 18 point Perpetua.
The illustrations are pencil and watercolor reproduced in full color.
10 9 8 7 6 5 4 3 2 1

Library of Congress Cataloging-in-Publication Data
Jung, Minna. William's ninth life / story by Minna Jung ; pictures by Vera
Rosenberry.   p.   cm.
"A Richard Jackson book"—Half-title.
Summary: William, an old cat who has lived happily with an old woman, is given a chance to
pick a new life for himself.
ISBN 0-531-05492-6.   ISBN 0-531-08642-9 (lib. bdg.)
[1. Cats—Fiction.   2. Old age—Fiction.]   I. Rosenberry, Vera,
ill.   II. Title.   PZ7.J954Wi   1993
[E]—dc20   92-44520

For my mother and father

——M.Y.

To my mother, Katherine

——V.R.

ILLIAM was a skinny cat with patchy gray fur and a crooked, very long tail.

Elizabeth was a skinny woman with thin gray hair that she combed into a crooked, very long braid.

The sea gave William to Elizabeth. When he was a tiny kitten, she saved him from a fisherman who was about to throw him into the waves.

In the years following, William and Elizabeth grew old together in their little cottage by the sea.

Elizabeth loved William more than anything or anyone.

William loved Elizabeth more than anything or anyone.

One day, William fell asleep on his favorite sunlit windowsill, the one that faced the sea.

He woke to the sound of a strange voice. "William," it called, again and again.

He was warm and comfortable, so he kept his eyes shut.

"Wake up, William!" The impatience in the voice roused him to open one eye.

Sitting next to him, he saw another cat, wonderfully strange-looking, with thick gray-green fur the color of the sea and large pointed ears.

When he saw the cat, William felt a queer silvery shiver flash through his old body. He stirred, and after a proper and delicious cat stretch . . .

in which he arched backwards,

and forwards,

he sat down neatly next to the gray-green cat.

The strange cat spoke first. "William," it said. "The time has come for you to choose your ninth life."

"I beg your pardon?" asked William politely.

"Your eighth life is drawing to a close. You must decide upon your new one—your ninth life. It will be your choice."

"Do I always choose my next life?" asked William.

"Yes. You have chosen eight times already. Cats do not remember their previous lives. They move on to each new life without looking back—until they come to the ninth. Your next life will be your last, William, so choose with care."

William was curious. "When my seventh life ended, did I choose Elizabeth?" he asked.

The strange cat shrugged as much as a cat can shrug. "You asked for a home by the sea. You asked for plants to chew on, and a hearth. You asked for love. We filled in the rest."

The strange-looking cat gazed at William with eyes like black polished stone. "This life turned out well, I see. But you are a cat, and all cats must complete the cycle of their nine lives."

William considered. The notion of having lived so many different lives was certainly exciting. But as the strange cat made an impatient noise through his nose, William did not hesitate any longer.

"I choose to remain here," he said to the gray-green cat.

The strange cat blinked. Then it seemed gently amused. "Nonsense," it said. "Cats do not choose to live an old life again."

"If I leave, Elizabeth will be alone," said William. "She is old, too. She needs me."

The gray-green cat sighed. "William," it said. "Cats are allowed to live again . . . and again . . . and again. Isn't that wonderful?" The strange cat leaned toward William. "There are so *many* choices," it purred dreamily.

William looked out to the sea. "I am old. My imagination fails me. I couldn't possibly choose, so this life is just fine for me, thank you."

The cat moved closer to William,

and it seemed to grow larger,

and larger,

until William felt as if he were drowning in gray-green fur the color of the sea.

He dimly felt a paw touch him, and he heard the words, "Choose, William."

The windowsill, the view of the sea, and the entire room dissolved into images that filled William's eyes.

He stood on a ship that smelled like tar and the
delicious inside of a tuna-fish can. He was a young cat, a
pirate cat on a galleon that rolled happily with the waves
and the songs of the sailors on board. A salty wind
crackled the sails and tickled his whiskers.

The strange cat nodded.

The vision changed suddenly. An Egyptian sun burned into William's eyes. And he found himself in a golden city bordered by desert sands. Three distant pyramids shimmered on the horizon, and William saw cats, cats everywhere. He even saw statues of cats, and dark-robed people bowing before them.

The strange cat smiled.

Then Egypt faded away, and William stretched out luxuriously on a satin cushion filled with soft feathers. He wore a green silk bow around his neck—a green, he felt proudly, that exactly matched his eyes. As a hand glittering with rings smoothed his fur, a servant placed before him a crystal dish heaped high with pink salmon.

The strange cat purred.

Faster and faster, a colorful map of William's choices spread out in his mind. He glimpsed dangerously exciting alleys in which cats sang by moonlight, lofty barns where cats dozed in the straw, summer fields humming with insects and rustling with cats on the prowl. . . .

Until William suddenly shut his eyes.

He remembered that yesterday Elizabeth had picked him up, hugged him, and said, "I love you, William, because you're skinny, ugly, and old—just like me."

He remembered how Elizabeth would stand on the beach, her skirts pinned up above the foaming sea, and catch fish for his dinner as he watched and waited a prudent distance from the waves.

He thought of their little cottage. It was shabby, to be sure, but sunlight and sea winds kept it always fresh and sweet.

He thought of sleeping on Elizabeth's pillow, where he could feel her snoring stir his fur.

When William opened his eyes, he was still sitting on the windowsill. The strange gray-green cat stood and stretched.

"Tomorrow," it said coolly, "you will fall into a deep sleep. Elizabeth will find you . . . dead."

"Dead!" William cried in horror.

"A death only in this life. You will have moved on to your ninth."

William thought sorrowfully of what his death would mean to Elizabeth.

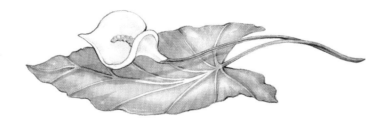

A minute ticked by, and then the strange cat spoke in sad puzzlement.

"William," it said. "This is a great gift. Cats have *always* had nine lives, and cats *always* move on until the cycle of their lives is complete. Cats *never* refuse their next life. You, William, are a cat. You will forget."

"That is the point," said William. "Forget Elizabeth? I must stay here."

The door to the cottage flew open then, and Elizabeth walked in. "William!" she called. "I'm back from the store."

She came to his window. She didn't appear to notice the strange cat at all, and scooped William into her arms. "Just come see what I have for your dinner!" she said to him.

As they went toward the tiny kitchen, William looked back. "I will ask for a home by the sea. I will ask for plants to chew on, and a hearth. I will ask for love." But the gray-green cat had vanished. "Wait!" William meowed.

Elizabeth stroked him and said, "Yes, William. I know. It's dinnertime."

The next day was wretched
for William.

He followed Elizabeth everywhere.

He wound himself tightly around her ankles
until she tripped.

He chewed all the plants until he got a stomachache.

He meowed whenever he managed to get Elizabeth's
attention, and he meowed when he didn't get her
attention.

He tried to tell her that today
he would be leaving forever.

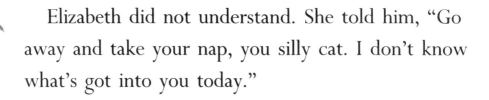

Elizabeth did not understand. She told him, "Go
away and take your nap, you silly cat. I don't know
what's got into you today."

Sleep was the last thing William wanted, because he knew he would never wake up with Elizabeth in their cottage again.

He tried desperately to stay awake.

He ran away
from drowsy sunbeams.

He hardly ate, hoping his
hunger would keep him alert.

He watched Elizabeth constantly.

But he felt sleepier and sleepier.

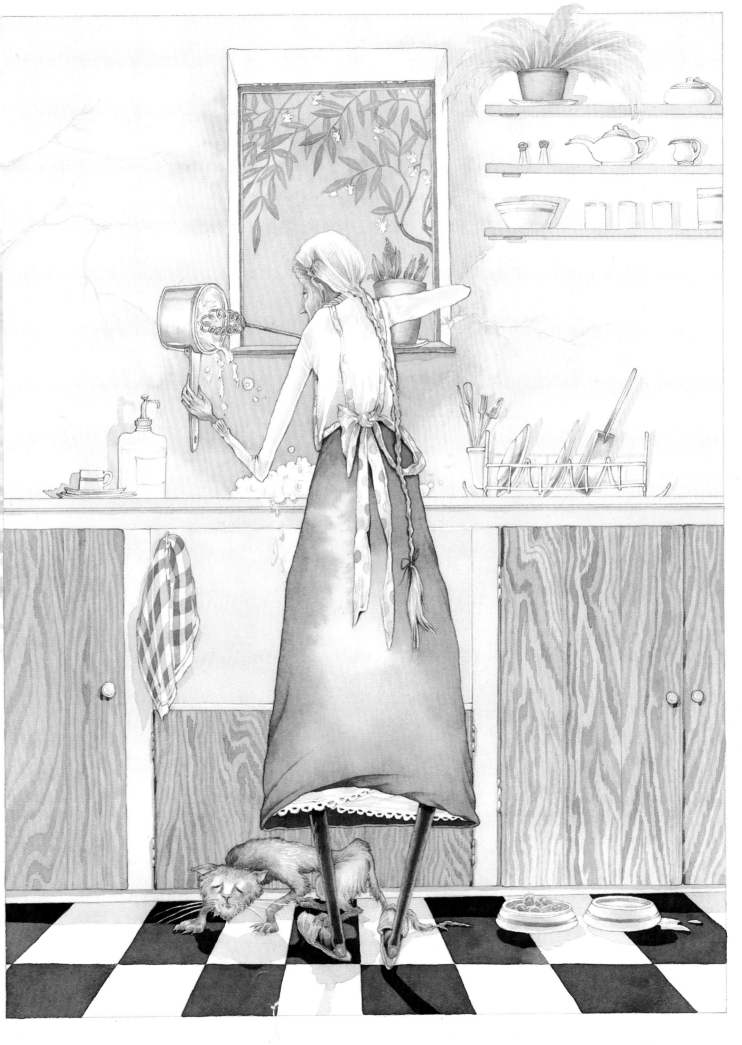

Somehow, he found himself on his windowsill in the late afternoon. The window was open a crack, and through it blew the windy smell of seaweed and salt.

Then, he knew. He looked at Elizabeth, nodding off in her rocking chair. He looked around at the little cottage, and he looked out at the gray-green wavy sea.

"Good-bye," William meowed sadly. An unbearable despair settled over him, and he lay down. But before he closed his heavy eyelids, he looked out at the sea and said quietly, "Please."

He fell asleep.

Several hours later, a cat woke up. A voice was calling, "William, where are you?"

The air was very dark. He did not know where he was, and stretched lazily.

He felt a sliver of cool wind in his fur.

He saw the glowing embers of a hearth.

He saw the ragged edges of plants that looked as if something—perhaps a cat—had chewed on them.

Through a window, he saw a starlit ocean.

Then he heard the old scratchy voice again. "William," it called. "Where are you? Come sleep on my pillow."

The voice sounded familiar. He was filled with a feeling of comfort and love.

"Thank you," the cat said politely. He did not quite know why he said it or whom he was thanking. But he jumped off the windowsill and went toward the voice.